...AND THEN THERE WERE DINOSAURS

by Sari Steinberg

Yellow Brick Road
PRESS Ltd.
St. Helier, Jersey

Art Studio: Scopus Productions
Art Director: Dick Codor
Sets and Models: Hedda Harari, Inbal Better
Photography: Reuven Atiya
Graphic Design: Benjie Herskowitz

ISBN: 0-943706-19-X

Printed in Hong Kong

Six Worlds Were Created Before Our World.

– Jewish Legend

Before God created the creatures of the Sixth World He turned to the Land of Israel for advice.

"What kind of creatures do you think should live on your land?" God asked.

The Land paused for a millennium or so to think.

"If I were You," she said, "I would make creatures of different shapes and different sizes, who eat different parts of different plants. That way they won't all want the same food, and they won't fight. If they are nice to each other, I promise to make sure there is enough food for them all."

"That seems reasonable," said God. And He pointed His finger and said:

"Let there be...

...D-I-N-O-S-A-U-R-S!"

And then there were dinosaurs.

Some were big and some were small.

Some walked on land.

Some swam in ponds.

Some flew in the sky.

The day the dinosaur world was complete, the Land had a golden glow about her.

"You've done a wonderful job, God," she beamed, as she watched the many different dinosaurs at work and at play.

The Land was enchanted by Diplodocus, as he reached
his long neck into the treetops to snatch a mouthful of leaves.

She marvelled as Coelurus dug holes with his
thin fingers, in search of edible roots.

She smiled as Stegosaurus collected seaweed on the spikes of her tail
and as Euoplocephalus cracked fallen coconuts with the hammer-like
end of his tail.

The Land giggled whenever Parasaurolophus drew her pointy face out of a berry patch and licked her juice-stained snout.

She was impressed by Triceratops, who could cut branches into bite-sized pieces with his sharp beak.

She didn't even mind being bopped on the head when Iguanodon dropped the fruits he hand-picked.

And she savored the moments when Dimetrodon hugged the ground while playfully eating wild grass.

Most of all, the Land loved Tyrannosaurus Rex. He was majestic and proud and brave. He stood on two legs and could look even giant Diplodocus in the eye – if Diplodocus bent his neck a little. Tyrannosaurus used his huge, strong teeth to rip chunks of tough, chewy bark from the trunks of trees.

"I will be good to these creatures," promised the Land. "I will flow with tree sap and dewdrops. I will grow lush grasses and luscious fruits. All the dinosaurs have to do is be good to each other, and I will be good to them."

For some 150 million years – give or take ten million – the dinosaurs were nice to each other. They swam, ran, jumped, climbed, slid, swung, and spun. In between, of course, they also ate, drank, slept, built nests, and brought more little dinosaurs into the world.

Then one day, Diplodocus saw a beautiful treetop that looked like a bright green cloud floating in the air. As he walked toward the tree, he didn't notice that Tyrannosaurus was munching on its bark.

Suddenly Tyrannosaurus roared, "This is MY tree!"

Diplodocus had never imagined that trees could belong to ANYBODY.
So he ignored Tyrannosaurus.

"He's just cranky," Diplodocus thought to himself. But as he reached the
tree, Tyrannosaurus sprang at him and bit him hard on the neck.

"Stop! Stop!" Diplodocus cried as he ran away. He ran and ran until he was sure he was safe.

Then, as he caught his breath, he suddenly realized, "If Tyrannosaurus can own a tree, so can I. I won't let anybody eat from my tree either." He wrapped himself around the nearest tree and shouted, for everyone to hear, "This tree is mine! Mine! MINE!"

The Land was worried about the selfish way the dinosaurs were behaving. But when it seemed that things were quieting down, the Land heaved a sigh of relief and relaxed.

Then Euoplocephalus came to Diplodocus' tree, looking for coconuts.

"This is MY tree," growled Diplodocus, and he whipped Euoplocephalus with his long tail.

Euoplocephalus went flying into a nearby pond. When he swam ashore, he did not run away. Instead, he yelled, "How dare you?!" and banged Diplodocus on the head with his own deadly tail.

Once again Diplodocus ran away, and Euoplocephalus took over his tree. But Diplodocus didn't give up. He claimed tree after tree, defending each tree against other dinosaurs until, finally, he had a small grove all to himself.

Before long all the dinosaurs began selfishly guarding trees and fields and ponds that they called their own. They fought off other dinosaurs with their horns their hands, their teeth, and their tails.

"This is terrible!" the Land called out to God. "Your creatures are hurting each other because of their selfishness!"

"Don't worry," God assured her. "Deep down, they are good. But we must find a way to teach them to be good to each other."

The Land agreed.

To teach the dinosaurs a lesson, she decided to grow less food. Some trees died, and some grasses stopped growing. The smaller ponds dried up, and the bushes grew fewer berries.

"Now they will learn to share," she told God, "because if they don't, they will all go hungry."

But instead of sharing, the dinosaurs became even more selfish.

When Triceratops' tree died, he stabbed Parasaurolophus and stole her berry patch.

When Coelurus ran out of fresh roots, he dug up Iguanodon's eggs and ate them.

And when Dimetrodon's field ran out of grass, he swallowed
Stegosaurus WHOLE and took over her pond.

And the fiercest of all, Tyrannosaurus Rex, killed dinosaur after dinosaur as he developed a taste for fresh red meat.

This was more than the Land could bear. Her favorite dinosaur had become her greatest disappointment. "Oh no! No! NO!" she cried. Then she grew angry. "These creatures have not learned anything about being nice to each other. They are meaner and more selfish every day. They must go!" she demanded.

This time God did not defend the dinosaurs. Sadly, He agreed that the time had come to end the Sixth World.

"Destroy these creatures!" God commanded the Land.

BARROOM!!!!

The Land shook and trembled furiously, splitting her crust into two, then three, then four, then hundreds of pieces. Thousands of the smaller dinosaurs fell into the cracks, never to be seen again.

The Land's volcanoes boiled and burst. The bigger, heavier dinosaurs could not escape the red-hot lava that came pouring out like a blanket over the Land.

The earthquakes let out poisonous gas, killing the creatures in the air. The volcanoes blew black ash into the sky, blocking the sun. The sky turned a charcoal gray. Without sunlight, the plants could not grow at all. The remaining dinosaurs had nothing to eat. And soon, they too died.

Exhausted, the Land fell silent. No more creatures were alive.

For about 65 million years, God was sad. The Land was lonely.

"Perhaps we should start again," said God one day.

"I'll create a Seventh World, with a special Seventh Day for resting and thinking. Maybe then the new creatures will have time to talk to each other. Maybe then they will solve their problems without fighting."

"That's a great idea," replied the Land, happy at the prospect of a new world. "Maybe this time You could create smart creatures who know right from wrong. Then they will understand why it is important to be good to each other."

God agreed.

With a star-like twinkle in His eye, God flashed His big rainbow smile, pointed at the Land, and said:

"Let there be...